HELEN NICKOLSON
GREAT GRANDMA'S SHED
MARCUM ROAD FOLLIES

ILLUSTRATED BY TANYA MANEKI

Great Grandma's Shed: Marcum Road Follies

Children's book
by
HELEN NICKOLSON

Illustrated
by
TANYA MANEKI

BOOKS

Adelaide Books
New York/Lisbon
2019

GREAT GRANDMA'S SHED: MARCUM ROAD FOLLIES
Children's book
By Helen Nickolson

Illustrated
By Tanya Maneki

Published by Adelaide Books, New York / Lisbon
adelaidebooks.org
Children's Literature Editor
Adelaide Franco Nikolic

For any information, please address Adelaide Books
at info@adelaidebooks.org
or write to:
Adelaide Books
244 Fifth Ave. Suite D27
New York, NY, 10001

ISBN-13: 978-1-950437-98-6
ISBN-10: 1-950437-98-1

Printed in the United States of America

For my daughter Katherine Eleanor Michel

Contents

Dear Readers,

While driving my daughter Katherine to day care about 28 years ago, I began telling her my "dreams" about Old Red, the kind convertible with magical powers who lived next to us in the country. He also had some adopted buddies–a Dalmatian called Cutie Pie and a duck named Teepo. These stories were very comforting to Katherine, especially when she didn't want to be separated from me. Years later, she still would oftentimes ask me if I had had a "dream," so I began recording the adventures of Old Red. Some of you will recognize characters in these stories, and I hope this will give you only sweet memories of a previous time. I especially hope that the little ones will enjoy having the stories read to them.

Sincerely,

Helen Nickolson

Old Red

Old Red lived in the small country town of Nicolaus, which was teensy in size but gigantic in heart. Nicolaus is in California, but not the beach or Hollywood parts that most people think of; instead it's a Northern California farming community of around 300 people, many of whom come from families that immigrated from Germany and Switzerland. A lot of rice, along with alfalfa and walnuts, is produced and exported from this area. Traffic backups rarely occur, but if one does, you can count on it being caused from tractors driving slowly down the road. And every so often, you're bound to see a couple of farmers in their pickups stopped in the middle of the road chatting about the latest community news.

This is a close-knit community that is very supportive of its schools, sports, and recreational facilities like its pool where generations of locals have taken swimming lessons. One of the primary fund-raising events for the schools is the annual Labor Day Parade and Picnic. The parade highlights tractors, antique cars, horses, and floats from different service groups, the three local grammar schools, and one high school. Sometimes a family designs and builds a theme-based float and has family members of all age groups riding on board. One of the best floats Katherine Michel's family ever entered was based on The Wizard of Oz, and that won the overall best entry in the parade! The four local schools rotate responsibility for money-making food venues–Pancake Breakfast, Hamburger Booth, Lunch Booth, and Dessert Booth—and they keep the money to use on special activities for their students. Yes, everyone becomes excited and involved and the event gets special coverage in the Appeal Democrat from the neighboring big city of Marysville (well, it's huge compared to Nicolaus).

Old Red loved his home because it wasn't very big, the town was sparsely populated, and he could roam the winding country roads as he pleased; after all, he was a spectacular, one-of-a-kind car. In the morning he would hear the birds chirp and at night he would sometimes hear coyotes. He often saw quail walking among shrubs and thought how adorable they were following their mother trustingly and being protected by their father at the rear. He also saw rabbits and squirrels and wild turkeys, but he didn't appreciate it when the wild turkeys tried to sit on him and made a little bit of a poopy mess. He didn't like that at all and honked loudly whenever they tried to do that again!

He slept in an old Swiss woman's shed, which was deep and narrow and had once been used as a chicken coop but was now a storehouse for all kinds of things—sometimes things that were spooky looking in the dark. He knew that the tall, old grandfather clock with a gold face was just that, but in the dark it sometimes looked like a medieval knight in full armor with a sword nearby. The dusty Halloween decorations included ghosts and goblins and spiders, and Old Red dreaded the thought of spiders crawling on him; that just made him shiver all over. Old Red was fearless, but he had to remind himself of that sometimes. He had been specially constructed, with the aid of some chips, by the Olive Grove Car Manufacturing Company to be courageous, daring, and multi-talented.

The old Swiss woman was well known by the children of Nicolaus, who called her Great-Grandma Erica, so Old Red began to affectionately call her Great-Grandma too after she began yodeling him to sleep every night. She was so gentle and would finish her yodeling with "Edelweiss" because she missed her native Alps and the white wildflowers that grew abundantly there. She would finish by lightly kissing him on his hood as if that were his forehead and then kindly pat the spot as if she could seal that kiss. He understood her nostalgia since he had felt a great deal of melancholy after his designer simply dropped him off by the roadside one day. Why that had happened he had no idea, no clue. Ah, but he really didn't want to think about that time since he treasured where he had finally arrived and enjoyed the Nicolaus countryside so much.

Although he loved all of the roads in Nicolaus, he loved the one he lived on the most because there weren't many houses around. But, the few houses that were there had children in them and these children were Old Red's best friends; they were his ever most special buddies! He especially loved Katherine who was his outstanding pal and lived next door. Old Red, however, had a gigantic heart with enough room for everyone he loved, which was a good thing because he loved everyone!

Oftentimes, when parents were too busy to take the children somewhere, Old Red would gather the little ones and drive them to wherever the parents wanted them to go. You see, the parents trusted Old Red to take their children to the zoo, the park, the local swimming pool, and just about anywhere. They knew he was extraordinary and that no car or person could ever replace him!! After all, where else would you find such a beautiful, long, red convertible which could expand like an accordion to fit as many children as necessary? Where else would you find a car with headlights that could see into the darkest corner, a grille whose grin was a mile wide, doors that could hear a peep, a horn that could speak, tires full of courage, and an engine full of wisdom? Everyone wholeheartedly agreed that Old Red was the most special car of all!

Well, one Saturday none of the parents was able to take the children to the movies and Katherine and her cousin Ellie really wanted to see the new movie "One Hundred and One Dalmatians." So, who came to the rescue? Trustworthy Old Red, of course!

First, he picked up his buddy Katherine and then zipped across the road for Sam, Katherine's best "boy" friend. They looped around to cousin Ellie's house and then stopped by for Annie, a little further down the road. Those were all the children on East Marcum Road in Katherine's class, and they each had very special talents! Since they were going to the movies in Yuba City he stopped by for Hailey, another one of Katherine's cousins who was very special indeed and who would soon be moving to Nicolaus. She fit right into the group!!!

So, they went to the movie theatre that peaceful Saturday. Old Red gave the children money for their tickets and for popcorn and one soda each. He told them to behave because he would be watching them from the parking lot with his bright x-ray eyes and listening with his sharp door-ears open. And all the children knew this was true because not only was Old Red very special but talented like no other car.

After the movie was over, the children walked through the lobby and there they saw a little dog that looked identical to the black-and-white spotted puppies they had just seen in "One Hundred and One

Dalmatians" tearfully hiding in the corner. Could she have jumped out of the screen? Was she hiding from the movie's villain, Cruella De Vil? The children's imaginations raced like a fast moving, boxcar shaking, rumbling train.

No, she wasn't from the movie but she was so cute! Poor little thing, she looked so scared and lonely that the children walked over to her. She yipped and yipped and they understood that she was lost. They felt so sad for her that they took her outside with them to ask Old Red if they could keep her.

Old Red didn't like the idea, but he thought it wouldn't hurt if she went for ice cream with them. His special treat to the children was to always take them out for ice cream after a movie. That was both his special treat and their special secret from the parents. So, they went to the ice cream parlor and, while Katherine, Sam, Ellie, Annie, and Hailey were inside, the puppy stayed with Old Red. Since they were alone, Old Red chatted with the baby Dalmatian and began to feel warm and loving toward her. She told him she had lost her parents and didn't have a home or anyone who cared for her. Old Red felt so sad to hear that that he told her she could live with him in Great-Grandma's shed. After all, she wouldn't take up very much space.

When the children came back, Old Red told them the little Dalmatian would stay with him and she would be called Cutie Pie. The children were so happy to hear that. They all laughed and hugged and kissed both Old Red and Cutie Pie. Old Red just chuckled and little Cutie Pie yipped all the way to Nicolaus where she finally gave her first yap of happiness when she saw her new home—Great-Grandma's shed.

Old Red and the Cows

Early one bright morning, Old Red and Cutie Pie heard a lot of commotion outside Great-Grandma's shed. Being late sleepers, they didn't like being awakened. The noise sounded like hooves pounding on grass and heads butting against trees and limbs being torn off. Every now and then there was a "moo, moo" and a "moo, moo, moo, moo" that was almost like laughter.

Cutie Pie and Old Red quickly hurried out of the shed to see what was happening and, of all things, it seemed like a cow party was going on. There were five cows prancing and dancing around Great Grandma's yard and they were having a GRAND old time! There was a brown and white spotted Guernsey, a Jersey cow with a white underside, a lovely golden Limousin, a black Angus, and a sweet looking Hereford. What could they be celebrating? Could they be having a cow convention?

But Great Grandma, in an old robe and white hair uncombed, was out there too and she wasn't one bit happy about the mess those cows were

making. She knew that they just didn't know any better, but, still, she didn't appreciate their frivolity at her expense. Of course, any reasonable person would feel the same way, and, kind though she was, she wasn't always reasonable. Yes, she did have a bit of a temper and a streak of stubbornness. Great Grandma liked things to be neat and clean and pretty and having anyone—much less cows—mess up her yard was not her idea of a proper party. She started chasing the cows, waving her arms and shouting, "Shoo, shoo, shoo. Get out of my yard. Shoo." The cows, however, were cow-like rude and didn't listen to her at all; instead, they just moo-moo-laughed and went on with their party.

Upon seeing this situation, Old Red and Cutie Pie thought they should help Great Grandma. So old Red started honking and Cutie Pie started yipping and they finally managed to scare the cows back to their pasture on Grandpa Leo's ranch. Good thing that the ranch wasn't far away and that they didn't have to cross Highway 99. That would have been too difficult even for Old Red.

Old Red and Cutie Pie thought the problem was taken care of until the same cows showed up again the next day mooing and dancing as if they were doing the Irish jig. But cows didn't dance the jig and these cows weren't Irish. Interestingly enough, for cows they were quite graceful and jumped high enough to click their heels. Losing her patience with them,

Great Grandma ran out again, waving and shouting but, again, the cows didn't pay any attention. Poor Great Grandma. She didn't deserve those irresponsible and disrespectful cows.

Old Red thought, "Wait a minute. This time we need to do something that will really scare those cows. But what can we do?"

Finally, he came up with an idea. He remembered that the old scary scarecrow that had scared millions of birds away every summer was standing against the left backside of the shed. He remembered how he himself had gotten a fear tickle across his back fender when he first saw Mr. Scarecrow. Remembering all this, he told Cutie Pie to borrow the clothes and dress up as Mr. Scarecrow. Cutie Pie got dressed and Old Red then drove Cutie Pie out of the shed very slowly until they could see the renegade, Irish jig-dancing, heel-clicking cows.

Once they had the cows in sight, Old Red accelerated and began honking. Scarecrow Cutie Pie began waving her arms and making such scary faces that the cows were totally startled. As a matter of fact, they were really so frightened that they managed to run home to Grandpa Leo's pasture in less than one minute. That probably was a world record!

Once more, Old Red and Cutie Pie thought the problem was taken care of and they felt so relieved until, believe it or not, the same cows showed up again the following day. Grandpa Leo's pasture food must have made those cows either really dull or plain fearless! It sure had made them into athletes!! Just like before, Great Grandma tried to chase the cows away but they didn't pay any attention. She yodeled at them "Shoo, shoo, shoo." And they yodeled right back, "Moo, moo, moo." It was like an outdoor concert in motion with the yodeling of "shoo, shoo, shoo," and "moo, moo, moo." The cows made the low notes of the contrabassoon and Great Grandma kept to the higher notes of the flute. Too bad that Katherine and the Marcum Road kids weren't around to witness the event, but they had all gone away to camp for the week.

Seeing how emboldened the cows had become, Old Red and Cutie Pie decided that they had gone too far!! These cows were taking advantage of a little old lady who was probably just a fraction of each individual cow's size. Shame! Shame! Shame! It was time to really take matters into their own hands and make sure the artistic, foolish cows would never return. With this in mind, Old Red and Cutie Pie came up with a wonderful scheme.

Old Red asked Cutie Pie to help him put on his black Spanish Fighting Bull costume (Old Red had dressed up as a bull the previous Halloween when he had taken the children trick-or-treating. Great Grandma, by the way, was a wonderful seamstress and had actually made the masterful costume for Old Red).

When Old Red finished dressing, he looked enormously muscled with dangerous long horns, and he looked MEAN! He looked so mean and aggressive that even he couldn't look at himself, so he stayed away from the full-length mirror in Great Grandma's shed. He told Cutie Pie to hide inside the costume and hold a burning torch above the bull outfit so that the cows would see the flames and smoke coming out through the top. He also told Cutie Pie to put on the special tape, which sounded like firecrackers exploding, that they stored in a safe place high up in the shed and brought out only for Fourth of July festivities.

They slowly rolled out of the shed until they could see the cows. Then, quick as a snap, Cutie Pie lit the torch and turned on the tape. Old Red lunged at the cows, bellowing, shrieking, and grunting like an angry bull. It was a sound coming from the gut that meant nothing would stand in his way. This time, the cows were so scared they could barely move, but they managed to get out of Old Red's way and they rushed home shaking with fear—again in record speed!

Watching the cows run, Old Red, Cutie Pie, and Great Grandma just laughed and laughed because they knew the cows would never return. And, sure enough, they never did. Because Old Red and Cutie Pie had been so courageous and creative, Great Grandma gave Cutie Pie a pink barrette for her hair and Old Red some of his favorite food: eggplant, squash, and corn.

Old Red and the Spaghetti Booth

It was a beautiful sunny morning in July and Old Red, Cutie Pie, and their new friend Teepo the duck had just gotten up. Old Red and Cutie Pie had met Teepo along Coon Creek earlier in the week when they had miraculously saved him from the coyotes and other vultures chasing him–but, that's another story. Anyway, they all made breakfast and went outside Great Grandma's shed to eat and enjoy the day. Suddenly, Old Red exclaimed, "I've been doing some thinking about Christmas and we need to make some plans!" Of course, Cutie Pie and Teepo were totally surprised and all they could do was to stare at Old Red. After all, what was he talking about? Christmas in July? Didn't he remember that Christmas was in winter?

Old Red realized by the looks on their faces that they didn't understand, so he explained further: "What I mean is that we need to make some money for Christmas so that we can buy presents for all the kids on Marcum Road. Last year at Christmas we couldn't buy anything really special and I don't want the same thing to happen this year!

Cutie Pie and Teepo perked up right away and said what a great idea that was. But then they stopped, thought for a while and said, "But Old Red, how are we going to do this? What can we do to make money?"

Old Red answered, "Well, I was thinking that we could have a booth and sell food to people going by. I don't know exactly what kind of food but we can come up with something."

So, the three of them sat around all morning and thought and thought and thought. They thought of a hot dog booth and a pizza booth and a hamburger booth but, each time, one of them didn't like the idea so they decided to keep on thinking.

Finally, Cutie Pie barked, "Yip, Yip, Yip. I have it. I have it!"

Teepo answered, "Quack, Quack, Quack" and Old Red went "Honk, Honk, Honk." They meant, "Tell us, tell us, tell us. We can't wait."

Then Cutie Pie said, "Let's have a spaghetti booth! We can put up a big sign on Grandpa Leo's property by Highway 99 so people will know how to find us and we can build a booth right by Great Grandma's driveway. We can make the spaghetti right here in our kitchen and carry it to the booth. It'll be easy and I know we can do it."

"But Cutie Pie," both Old Red and Teepo answered, "We've never made spaghetti. We don't even know where to start. We've only TASTED spaghetti."

"That's OK," said Cutie Pie. "We can learn. Katherine's mom and dad can teach us. They live just next door, so let's go ask them."

Old Red and Teepo agreed to that and the three went to Katherine's house. They knocked on the door and spoke with Larry, Katherine's dad. Larry thought they had a great idea and he called to Katherine and her mom to also listen to the plans. When Katherine heard about the spaghetti booth she jumped up and down with excitement. Helen, Katherine's mom, also liked the plan but she didn't say much because she sensed that the three had come over to also ask a favor of her.

Sure enough, within a few minutes they did ask. At first, they hemmed and hawed but, finally, Cutie Pie blurted out, "Would you teach us how to make spaghetti?"

"No problem," Katherine said immediately. Then she looked at her mom and dad. Her parents just laughed and everyone knew it was okay.

The next day, Old Red, Cutie Pie, and Teepo went to work. They woke up early and built the booth. All of the kids who went by stopped and helped for a while. Sam was really helpful because that's just how he was; Ellie had great ideas how to organize the booth; Andrea gave some finishing touches and Hailey, who had stayed overnight with Katherine, laughed so much she had everyone laughing with her. When everything was finished, they painted a spectacular sign with bright, bright colors and glued some sparklers around the border.

The following day everyone gathered at Katherine's house to make spaghetti. Cutie Pie and Teepo first took a bath so they wouldn't make the house dirty. They knew that Katherine's mom was really particular about a clean house—especially about the kitchen and bathroom. Since Old Red was too big for the house, he used his tricks to shrink himself so that he could be placed on the kitchen counter and watch from there.

Katherine's mom and dad brought out all the ingredients for spaghetti sauce. They sautéed the meat, chopped onions and mushrooms, cut tomatoes and then put everything into a big pot so that the sauce would simmer. Once in a while, they would taste the sauce and add a few spices. After slowly simmering for a few hours, the sauce was ready so they boiled some spaghetti noodles, spooned sauce on top, and added shredded cheese.

It was SO good that everyone had two helpings, but there was enough left over for Old Red, Cutie Pie, and Teepo to use in their booth the next day. And they did use it the following day. The booth was BUSY. So many people stopped by that all the sauce was used by five o'clock in the evening.

Since the sauce was gone, Old Red, Cutie Pie, and Teepo made a new batch in their own kitchen in Great Grandma's shed. When they finished, the sauce looked great but when they tasted it, there was something wrong. It was much too salty! They felt so disappointed but didn't know what to do, so they went back to Katherine's house and asked her mom to help them. They looked so forlorn that Katherine's mom felt sorry for them, and she made a double batch of spaghetti and gave it to them.

This time the sauce lasted for two days. When the sauce was gone, they went right to work and made a new batch, which looked great. They tasted this new batch and started to sputter and choke. The spaghetti sauce had so much pepper that it took them one hour of drinking milk to calm down! Although their mouths felt better, Old Red, Cutie Pie, and Teepo felt really sad and disappointed in themselves. They had had such lofty dreams of buying wonderful Christmas presents for everyone, but now, they just didn't know what to do next.

Then they saw Katherine walking toward them and told her what had happened. While they were telling her the story, they started to cry and she, seeing how devastated they were, started to cry also. But then she stopped. She had an idea. She knew her mother couldn't help them anymore but she thought she herself might be able to.

"Hold on," she said. "I have a plan. I've watched my mom and dad make spaghetti sauce many times and I'm sure I can make it myself."

Everyone's face brightened. Why not try again with Katherine's help? They all agreed it was a great idea and started a new batch of sauce immediately. When they finished, they felt a little nervous but they got spoons and slowly tasted the sauce. A wonderful and satisfied look appeared on their faces. THE SPAGHETTI SAUCE WAS BETTER THAN KATHERINE'S MOM'S.

From that day until summer ended, Katherine helped Old Red, Cutie Pie, and Teepo make spaghetti each evening. The booth was a great success and everyone was pleased.

Christmas came and on Christmas day Old Red, Cutie Pie, and Teepo had special presents for all the kids on Marcum Road and a few others. Ellie received a lavender purse; Annie received a hat; Sam got a special shirt; Hailey got a sweatshirt; and Katherine, who had helped sooooo much, received a lovely pink ballerina dress from her special friends.

Christmas Wonderland

It was a hot day in July. The fireworks and parties for the Fourth were long gone, and the Marcum Road kids were bored but had no energy to do anything. It was just too hot–probably the hottest summer ever. Old Red knew how they felt, so he cranked up the ice-fan-umbrella-moisturizer in his mid-section so that the umbrella covered his car-body entirely. Inside the umbrella he had installed a battery fan that misted ice water very gently and moisturized everyone who sat within Old Red. So, he, along with Cutie Pie and Teepo, went and picked everyone up. By driving around, they could at least stay cool and eat soft, yummy chocolate ice cream since it wouldn't melt under the ice-fan-umbrella-moisturizer.

The coolness made them think of Christmas. Christmas had been absolutely wonderful to the kids on Marcum Road, Old Red, Cutie Pie and Teepo. Everyone had enjoyed the caroling, decorations, special cookies, and especially the presents. They remembered the presents peaking out

under a green Christmas tree that smelled so delicious and was loaded with decorations and tinsel and all kinds of bright things.

They remembered that on Christmas Day lights were shining everywhere and trees twinkled in the homes. Those trees were so beautiful! They were pure and fresh and covered with ornaments. Situated in a special spot where everyone could see it, each tree seemed to promise wonderful things to come and to bless each child who walked by and uttered a soft "ahhh."

They were all fondly remembering their Christmas holiday as they drove around Nicolaus that hot July day. They were chuckling about all the sweets they had eaten when suddenly, Cutie Pie almost fell out of Old Red.

"What happened Old Red? Why did you stop like that?" Cutie Pie yipped as she rubbed some bruised spots on her paws.

"I'm sorry Cutie Pie," Old Red answered. "I couldn't help myself when I saw that dried shell of a Christmas tree just lying in the ditch. The trees were so beautiful, but as soon as Christmas was over no one appreciated them anymore. Here it is July and that poor tree still hasn't been taken to a proper home where it can be recycled in some way."

When Cutie Pie heard this, tears started rolling down her eyes and she softly moaned, "Wuff, wuff, wuff..." What she meant was that this was awfully sad and that she wanted to do something about it. The trees deserved better treatment.

They all thought and thought and finally Old Red said, "I have it, everyone. I know what we can do, but everyone has to help and has to believe that this plan will work. First, we have to drive around and pick up any old Christmas trees that have just been dumped." And that's exactly what they did. They drove around Nicolaus and Yuba City and Marysville picking up all the used Christmas trees they could find. The trees looked so scraggly that it seemed pointless to pick them up, but Old Red had a plan. By the time they got back to Great-Grandma's shed they had gathered nineteen trees and Old Red had expanded to become as big as he could be–the size of a large bus.

They took the trees out and Old Red told the kids to start digging holes. No one complained although it was still really hot, but they did take a lot of breaks sitting under the ice-fan-umbrella-moisturizer and drinking the lemonade Cutie Pie and Teepo made. It took them all afternoon but, by the time the sun was just starting to go down, the holes were finished. In the meantime, Old Red had searched in the back of Great Grandma's shed, and he had found what he was looking for: a leather pouch with sparkling sprinkles inside. He hadn't used these sprinkles in many, many years and had almost forgotten about them.

He brought the pouch out to the holes and put three crystals in each of the 19 holes. As he did this, he said each time, "Oh beautiful tree, grow, grow, grow. Make this into a winter wonderland." He then told the kids to plant the trees.

As you can imagine, everyone was surprised but they did as Old Red had ordered. He noticed their confusion and explained that the crystals had magical powers and would work to make the trees grow again. The kids didn't really believe him, and knowing that, he told them they would just have to come back and check every week.

Sure enough, the kids did go back every week. The first few weeks they didn't see anything different but by the fourth week they saw tiny, fresh leaves sprouting from the branches. And, as time went on, more and more leaves developed so that by the following Christmas the trees had become truly magnificent.

That Christmas Old Red, Cutie Pie, Teepo, and the kids decorated the nineteen trees. Great-Grandma's back yard had become a winter wonderland, and every Christmas from that time on the friends got together and celebrated the magical Christmas wonderland they had created.

Old Red the Grump

One day, Old Red was practicing stopping, starting, turning right and left quickly, and backing up in Katherine's walnut orchard. He didn't have much to do that day so he thought it would be a great opportunity to improve his driving skills. Every once in a while, Katherine's dad would shout, "Hey, watch it, Old Red! Don't hit the walnut trees."

Of course, Old Red never hit the trees and he knew that Katherine's dad was just joking. Once in a while Old Red would get really close to one of the trees just to see the dad's reaction. And, sure enough, there was always a reaction!

That day Katherine's mom was out in the orchard too and she was talking about the garden they should plant that summer. Old Red overheard her say, "It sure looks like we had better plant a few more rows of eggplant and corn and more squash too. That Old Red eats a lot and that's his favorite food. Sometimes I can't believe how much that car eats."

When Old Red heard that, he wondered what she meant. Could it be that she thought he ate too much? Was he causing everybody a lot of trouble? Didn't they care about him or were they tired of having him around? The more that Old Red thought, the sadder he became. Tears slowly rolled down his lights as he went back to Great-Grandma's shed.

Cutie Pie immediately saw that something was wrong and she finally got Old Red to tell her what had happened. She couldn't believe that Katherine's mom had meant anything bad, but she couldn't convince Old Red to go over and talk about it. Instead, Old Red thought it best to not bother Katherine's mother and to just leave.

"But where will you go, Old Red?" Cutie Pie asked.

"I'm not sure, but I think I could get a job with a circus," Old Red answered. "There I could make some money and buy as much eggplant, corn, and squash as I want. Then I wouldn't bother anyone."

So Old Red started packing his things: pictures of the Marcum Road kids and souvenirs from all the places they had gone together. The more he packed, the more he cried. It was just all very sad and Cutie Pie couldn't stand to watch what was going on.

She ran over to Katherine's house and barked until Katherine and her mom and dad came out. They were amazed when they heard about Old Red's plans. Katherine's mom said, "This just doesn't seem like Old Red.

He's usually the most reasonable of everyone here but, now, it sounds as if he's become a little goofy. I'm going to go and talk with him."

She went to Great-Grandma's shed and there she found Old Red still crying. At the same time, she noticed some strange things, so she started questioning Old Red. She found that he had been staying up really late and hadn't had much sleep for a week. He hadn't been eating properly and hadn't taken his vitamin pills or his fluoride. And, he hadn't been brushing his grill regularly or washing his body.

By this time everyone from Marcum Road knew about Old Red and had decided to check on him. So, they all gathered at Great-Grandma's shed. Poor Old Red was feeling kind of embarrassed but he didn't need to worry because everyone loved him so much. They just laughed and said, "Old Red, it doesn't matter how old or how young you are. You still have to take care of yourself or you'll become a grump. We know from personal experience."

Teepo, who had been away on a short vacation to the town of Verona by the Feather River, waddled in. He had missed all the excitement, so Cutie Pie filled him in. Teepo, shaking his beak from side to side, looked at Old Red and said, "We're so used to you being strong and wise that we forget you might need us to watch out for you some times. Tomorrow I'm going to take you in for a full check-up at Dr. Kar's and then for a spruce-up at

AutoShine's and then for a refreshing afternoon dip in Coon Creek where we can enjoy a few slugs and worms."

Old Red just looked at Teepo very fondly and thought to himself, "A nice day out would be great, but I think I'll pass on the dip, the slugs, and the worms."

By then it was about time for everyone to leave so Katherine's dad walked up to Old Red and placed two things on him: one box of eggplant, corn, and squash, and a gold medal, which said "Grump of the Month."

Old Red and School Pranks

When the kids on Marcum Road were old enough to go to school, Old Red often drove them there. It was called Marcum Illinois School and it had about one hundred children ranging from kindergarten to the eighth grade. If he had to take only one or two children, Old Red remained his normal size. But, if he had to take the whole group, he would just make himself bigger until all the kids could fit in. Of course, Cutie Pie and Teepo always went along too.

One week, for some reason, the kids decided to play jokes on Old Red. First, on Monday during recess, Katherine phoned Old Red and told him she had a tummy ache. So, Old Red went to pick her up, but when he got there she started laughing and said, "Oh, Old Red, I'm fine. I was just teasing. You know I don't get tummy aches anymore."

On Tuesday, Sam called Old Red and said that a flying kite had hurt Ellie. Again, Old Red went to school to take Ellie home but Ellie was just fine! The kids laughed and said, "Ha, Ha, Old Red, we fooled you again."

Then on Wednesday, Ellie and Andrea called and said that they had fallen into muddy water after going down the slide, and they needed to change their clothes. One more time patient Old Red drove to school and, again, everything was just fine. The kids laughed and laughed when they saw him.

The final straw for Old Red came on Thursday when Hailey decided to call and also try to fool Old Red. Her story was that she had kicked the ball too hard during recess and sprained her toe and then that she had fallen during lunch and actually broken the same toe. Poor Old Red was suspicious when he heard this since it sounded pretty far-fetched, but he knew Hailey was accident-prone so he immediately drove to Marcum Illinois.

When he reached Marcum, Katherine, Ellie, Andrea, Sam, and Hailey were all there to greet him. Again, they laughed. They were really proud of themselves and didn't notice the glare on Old Red's grille; they didn't notice that his lights went on bright when he heard them laughing; they didn't notice that his color turned redder than red. They were too young to realize that Old Red had had enough of their pranks.

As a matter of fact, Old Red was becoming quite angry with all of them. He said to Cutie Pie and Teepo, "I have had enough jokes played on me and now I'm going to teach those kids that it's not nice to play mean jokes. I have always taken care of them, been nice to them, listened to their problems, pampered them on special days, cried with them, gone to every school function, and now they're taking advantage of me. I sure hope they're not acting this way toward their parents!"

Cutie Pie questioned, "But what are you going to do, Old Red?"

Teepo, who of the three was the most short-tempered, suggested that they just dump the kids into Coon Creek and then let them walk home. Of course, Teepo wasn't really serious since he knew Old Red would never do anything to endanger the children.

Old Red thought and thought and finally said, "You'll see what I'll do when we pick them up from school."

As usual, Old Red, Cutie Pie, and Teepo were waiting for the kids after school. After all the kids were gathered around him waiting to get inside, Old Red told them that they were going home in a little different manner that day. They didn't understand what he meant so he explained that, because they had behaved so badly toward him, they were going to walk home and they weren't going to stop by Perozzi's or Barker's for a snack.

The kids were shocked! Could this be the same Old Red who had never said a mean word to them? They moaned and groaned and groaned and moaned. They thought about crying to get some sympathy, and they thought about calling their parents but knew they would be in trouble if they explained the entire story. Finally, they accepted the fact that they had no choice but to walk, so they started walking with Old Red, Cutie Pie, and Teepo following closely behind. They walked and walked and walked.

Old Red felt sorry for them but he wouldn't let them ride. A few trickles ran down his windshield a couple of times and he felt very sad. Cutie Pie, and even Teepo, felt sad too. Old Red didn't want to see the children suffer, but he knew that if he gave in they would just take advantage of him again. Finally, after what seemed forever, they all reached home but were so tired–including Old Red, Cutie Pie, and Teepo–that they didn't even want to eat or talk. They just went straight to bed without eating dinner or watching TV.

The next morning, Old Red went by to pick up the kids. He wasn't sure what to expect, so he was really happy that each one of them said, "I'm sorry Old Red. I love you, and I won't play mean tricks on you or anyone again."

Old Red just answered, "Toot, Toot," that meant, "I love you too."

Old Red and Cutie Pie Rescue
Teepo the Mallard Duck

After having lived with Old Red and Cutie Pie for about a year, Teepo the Mallard duck suddenly rasped nasally but quietly in a stutter, "Would you please tell me how you saved me. I was so little and I just can't remember what happened and…I'm having such nightmares…I'm having a hard time sleeping…all I imagine are dark shapes chasing me and growling…oh, please, please, please tell me so that I can face these monsters that are chasing me."

Old Red and Cutie Pie gave each other a look that indicated they were shocked at their insensitivity to poor little Teepo. They hadn't realized that he was going through a bad period and needed their help to get over the terrifying experience he had had with the coyotes and other vultures along Coon Creek when they had miraculously saved him. He must have had amnesia for a while but now bits and pieces were coming back to him and scaring him throughout the night.

They probably should have realized because they had each seen a sad look in Teepo's eyes occasionally, but he covered up any gloominess very quickly and stayed close to them, so they didn't pay much attention. He liked to have them in his sight at all times since he was a sociable creature, but they had seen him wander off sporadically—which was very unlike him.

Thinking back, Old Red and Cutie Pie remembered that they had gone on a picnic on Coon Creek one hot summer day with the idea that they might take a dip in the water since it was over one hundred degrees Fahrenheit. Nicolaus regularly had very hot summer days and Great Grandma's shed didn't have air conditioning. Her house may not have had air conditioning either since she believed in thrifty living.

So, there they were on the water edge of Coon Creek when they saw a brown golden eagle with a huge wingspan descend on a mama mallard who had had ducklings only moments before. That golden eagle, one of the swiftest creatures on earth, swooped in on the mama mallard so quickly, knocking her unconscious and carrying her off in his talons, that Old Red and Cutie Pie could only stare in amazement. There was nothing they could do!

But then they saw the little duckling that the eagle had missed, and they also saw two husky lead coyotes running toward the creek howling as loudly as a full pack. A fox appeared briefly by the creek but ran off upon seeing the coyotes. Old Red, with the bushy coyotes charging into him, pulled the duckling onto his front seat before the hungry coyotes could reach it, and Cutie Pie covered it with her body. They were the first things that Teepo saw, and Teepo immediately identified with them as his family, thinking he was both a red car and a Dalmatian. Later, he tried to both bark and honk but the sounds he made sounded more like "teeepooo," so they named him Teepo.

Anyway, Teepo fit in with their lifestyle and ate the fruit and vegetables that Old Red really liked. They learned quickly not to give him any bread since it caused him to gain weight too quickly and didn't provide him with the nutrition he needed. Once, he became much too heavy and they had to put him on a diet! Since he was omnivorous, he was able to share in Cutie Pie's food also. He even liked the peanut butter that Cutie Pie loved so much, but he had to be careful to mix it in with something else so he wouldn't choke. He also knew to always have water nearby whenever he ate.

Luckily for Teepo, Coon Creek was just yards away from Great Grandma's shed so he could spend a lot of time in the water. He loved to dabble on the surface of the water and pick out fish for food at his leisure. He would sometimes sleep right on the water and wasn't afraid of eagles since they also sleep at night. He also greatly enjoyed the rice fields in the area since he could munch on duck-yummy insects and worms. When he described his favorite worm desserts to the Marcum Road kids, they would try to politely look away but sometimes they couldn't quite hold their food down. Teepo finally realized that this was not a good topic. THANK GOODNESS!

Yes, Teepo was growing up both physically and mentally and his understanding and empathy toward children and friends was increasing dramatically. Old Red and Cutie Pie were proud of Teepo for maturing nicely and really weren't that surprised that he was asking them about his beginnings and his rescue. He deserved an answer and so they began their story.

"Teepo, your mother had just given birth to you and everything would have been all right if a natural predator, the golden eagle, hadn't attacked her. We couldn't help her, but we were able to help you. What you're remembering are the coyotes and foxes that came after you. Yes, they were growling fiercely and their teeth were bared, BUT what you really need to remember is that we made sure you were safe and sound, AND you also really need to remember that we will always be here to help you and protect you. We love you, as do all the Marcum Road kids. Now, let's call them all over and let's all take a nap together. We promise that you will no longer have bad dreams!"

The Marcum Road kids all came over, heard what had taken place, and planted a kiss on Teepo's round-tipped bill. Each one gave him advice on having good dreams and Katherine related her best dream, which was about flying. She cherished the feeling of floating above the earth, or breezily soaring over valleys and lakes. She felt powerful and weightless like Super girl and only wished she could have that dream more often.

Teepo heartily chuckled nasally through his bill and said, "Katherine, you're talking to the wrong car-dog-duck here. Remember, that's what I do every day. I only wish I could put you on my wings and fly you wherever you wish. If only I could expand and contract like Old Red."

"Okay Teepo," Katherine replied. We, as a group can come up with a better approach for you. We just need to think for a few minutes." So, they huddled together and finally shouted "Eureka" in unison.

They were so excited that their words tripped over each other's. Finally, Hailey got them to calm down and they took turns explaining. She started with, "You need to put yourself in somewhat of a trance—kind of like self-hypnosis."

Sam followed with, "Imagine yourself at your strongest and most fearless."

Ellie added, "Accept that you're more cunning and smarter than any coyote or fox."

"Be ready to stare anything down," shouted Annie and accentuated that with a little kick that she had recently learned in hop-dance classes.

Katherine made the final exclamation by scrunching up her lips, standing on her toes, and discharging considerable dribble. Her message was "Spit at them!"

THE END

CPSIA information can be obtained
at www.ICGtesting.com
Printed in the USA
LVHW070748210221
679525LV00007B/220